16 SEP 2008 2/08

15 AUG 2008

14 OCT 2008

05 DEC 2008

30 JUL 2010

This book should be returned/renewed by the latest date shown above. Overdue items incur charges which prevent self-service renewals. Please contact the library.

Wandsworth Libraries
24 hour Renewal Hotline
01159 293388
www.wandsworth.gov.uk Wandsworth

Text and Illustrations copyright 2004 Hedley Griffin.

Hedley Griffin has asserted his rights to be identified as the author and illustrator of this work under the Copyright, Designs and Patents Act, 1988.

Published in 2004 by DangerSpot Books Ltd.
Old Bank House,
High Street,
Laxfield,
Woodbridge,
Suffolk.
IP13 8DX.

Printed by Proost NV, Turnhout, Belgium.

ISBN 0-9546565-1-2

The Hair-Raising Kite Flight

Hedley Griffin

DangerSpot Books Ltd.

'Look at the way those leaves are circling around the garden,' said Harey Rabbit, one autumn morning. He and his friends, Scampi the cat, and Chips the dog, were sweeping up the fallen leaves.

As Harey stepped back he became tangled up in a bed sheet on the washing line.

'Help! Help!' Harey cried. 'I'm being attacked by a scary monster, and it's going to eat me up!'

He rolled about, flapping and wrapping himself amongst the linen. The more he panicked the more he became knotted within the sheet.

'Help! I can't breath!' came the muffled voice from inside the monster. Scampi and Chips started to unwrap the sheet from around Harey as he popped his head out.

'Cor! That's better!' Harey sighed with relief. 'I could have been *stufflocated*!'

'Don't you mean *suffocated*, you hare-brained rabbit?' advised Scampi, giggling and releasing him from the scary bed-sheet.

'Look. All the leaves are running around the garden again,' said Harey.

'Every time we get them into a pile the wind blows them away again.

It's all very annoying!'

'Let's collect up all the leaves and put them on the compost heap,' suggested Scampi, placing them in the wheelbarrow.

'That's a good idea!' said Chips. 'Then, when they've rotted down they won't be able to fly away again, will they?'

'No, Chips!' sighed Scampi. 'How can a dog be so silly?' she thought.

'I've got an armful here,' said Harey, as he rushed off down the garden.

'And I've got at least three or four,' said Chips, following him with almost as many leaves. Chips could never add up and was always confusing his numbers.

Harey had so many leaves in his arms he could not see where he was going, which was very silly. He immediately stepped on a rake, which sprung up and hit him in the face. Bang!

'Arghh! Ouch!' he cried, as leaves flew everywhere and Harey fell on his back, hitting his head on the ground.

'You hare-brained rabbit!' scolded Scampi. 'You should look where you are going!'

'Who's a hare-brained rabbit, then?' said Pillow the parrot.

Harey lay on his back, looking at the sky.

'I can see hundreds of stars!' he said.

'I'm not surprised,' said Scampi, laughing. 'They're in your eyes, because you banged your head.'

'I know! Shall we go and fly our kite?' asked Harey.

'In this strong wind it'll go very high!'

'Can I hold the string, this time?' asked Chips.

'Yes, ok, Chips, but only if you promise not to let go,' said Scampi.

'I'll go and get it!' said Harey, rushing off like a hare-brained rabbit as usual.

In no time at all, he was back with the kite. The wind was strong indeed.

Harey held onto the kite as best he could, but he was being lifted off the ground.

'Help! Quick! Catch me. I'm flying away!' he yelled.

Chips held onto Harey's leg and Scampi held onto the other.

'It's going up in the air for miles and miles!' shouted Harey, excitedly.

'Whey-hey!'

'Don't let go of the string, Harey. We'll lose the kite!' said Chips.

'Don't let go of me, then!' cried Harey.

Just then a gust of wind took off and pulled them down the garden, through the gate, and into the field next door.

'Whey-Hey!' shouted Harey again. 'This is great! Don't let go of me!'

'We've got you!' said Scampi, as both she and Chips held onto Harey's legs.

They ran down the field as the wind and the kite pulled them further away from the house. Harey, Scampi and Chips did not know, but they were being pulled towards an electricity pylon, which was very dangerous.

Suddenly, the kite flew into the electricity cable.

There was a big flash of light and a loud explosion.

The three of them collapsed on the ground, shocked and burnt.

Luckily, for some strange reason,

they were not burnt too badly,

but they had to stay in bed for many weeks.

That was the biggest shock of all.

Place the DangerSpot stickers around your home as a reminder of the dangers and keep your children safe!

Don't allow children to play near electricity pylons, power stations, or railway lines.

Always keep an eye on young children at play. They depend on you for their safety.

Fit window locks and remove furniture away from windows to prevent children falling out.

A young child can easily suffocate or choke. Avoid letting them play with small objects.

Keep medicines, bleach, turps, caustic soda, etc. locked away or out of children's reach.

Remind children of areas of glass in doors and side panels, which could cause serious injury.

Avoid children being scalded by taking extra care with hot water, tea, coffee or soup, etc.

Always put in cold water first when running a child's bath and then add the hot.

Never leave sharp tools around and keep them away from children.

Guard all fires and heaters, especially open fires.

Information supplied by The Royal Society for the Prevention of Accidents. www.rospa.com